Which Wolf?

Adaptation by Emily Bouchard
Illustration by Georgia Lesley

978-1-952106-59-0 (paperback)
978-1-952106-57-6 (workbook)
978-1-952106-58-3 (ebook)

[Author's note: This children's book is an adaptation of a meaningful story often used in sermons and other inspirational venues. The story of the "Two Wolves" is a popular legend of unknown origin, sometimes attributed to the Lenape or Cherokee people.]

Connor and Sophie always love visiting their grandfather. They help him in his garden full of flowers and fresh veggies, and he tells them interesting stories from when he was young.

Connor wanted to stay in the garden, but his mother reminded him that he needed to finish his homework. He didn't want to go inside, but Grandfather made it easier by saying that Connor could use his big computer.

Connor felt important as he sat at that big desk and in that big chair. But it was hard for Connor to pay attention and sit inside by himself.

Grandfather noticed, came inside and pulled down a small stuffed animal – a little wolf – that Connor and Sophie often played with during their visits. He handed it to Connor, saying:

"Let this wolf help you concentrate and learn."

Connor went back to his math problem while holding the toy wolf in his lap.

Sophie is two years younger than Connor and loves playing with her big brother. She peeked into grandfather's office to see what Connor was doing, and when she saw the little wolf stuffie in his lap, she ran up to him squealing: "My turn! Catch me if you can!" snatching the toy and running out of the room.

Connor ran after her and grabbed the little stuffed wolf, but she didn't let go. They began to tug and pull, and pull and tug, until they both heard a terrible *RRRRRRRRRRIP!!!* They watched in dismay as stuffing flew everywhere.

Connor and Sophie stared at the mess they created. Sophie burst into tears and ran out of the room, yelling, "MOMMMMMMMMM!!! Connor ruined grandpa's stuffie!"

Connor turned and saw his grandfather standing by the door, motioning for Connor to come and sit by him. Connor shuffled over, head down, and sat at his feet.

After what seemed like a very long time, Connor looked up and was relieved when he saw a look of understanding in those wise old eyes. Grandfather smiled at Connor and asked, "Can I share a story my grandfather told me when I was your age?"

4

In a quiet voice Connor said, "Yes, please."

Grandfather thought back to that time and began:

"'A fight is going on,' my grandfather said to me. 'It is a fight between two wolves. One is all about fear - it is selfish and mean and full of hate.'"

Connor sat up, listening carefully.

Grandfather continued. "My grandfather told me, 'The other wolf is all about love - it is respectful, generous, and full of grace.'"

Connor imagined the wolves fighting in a forest, then he asked:

"Where were they fighting?"

"Believe it or not," grandfather said, "They are fighting inside you."

"Inside *me*?!" Connor was shocked!

"And inside me," grandfather added. "This same fight is going on inside everyone."

8

Connor's eyes got wide. He pictured wolves fighting inside himself AND inside everyone he knew, and everyone he didn't know, too!

Connor was full of curiosity and wonder when he asked, "Which wolf will win?"

Grandfather got a faraway look in his eyes, remembering that he asked the same question all those years ago. He looked down at Connor and shared what his grandfather told him...

"The one that wins is the one that you feed."

Connor wasn't sure he understood the story, but he felt better. That was, until he looked over at the mess on the floor and felt a rush of anger that the toy wolf was ruined. He looked back at his grandfather and then at his chest and began to think. And think. And think. Connor sat and thought some more as he tried putting the stuffing back inside the torn toy. He carried the two pieces carefully into the kitchen to show Sophie and to apologize.

But before saying anything, Connor saw Sophie playing

with his train set. He heard thoughts in his head that were loud and not very nice:

"Wait a minute, that's your favorite train! She knows you don't like her playing with it!"

He stomped towards Sophie, ready to take the train from her hands, but stopped himself, imagining the two wolves.

While he stood there watching her, the mean wolf was hissing to him, *"She shouldn't be playing with YOUR train! You have to get it back quickly before she breaks it!"*

Connor was ready to shout at his sister, but then he heard the other, kind wolf, even though it was much quieter: *"If she is enjoying playing with your train, and treating it well, you could join her and play with her, taking turns, and have fun together."*

Connor felt warm in his chest and stood up a little straighter, beginning to understand how he feeds the wolves!

He sat next to Sophie. "Can I play with you?" he asked, picking up some train tracks.

"Sure," Sophie said, handing Connor his favorite engine.

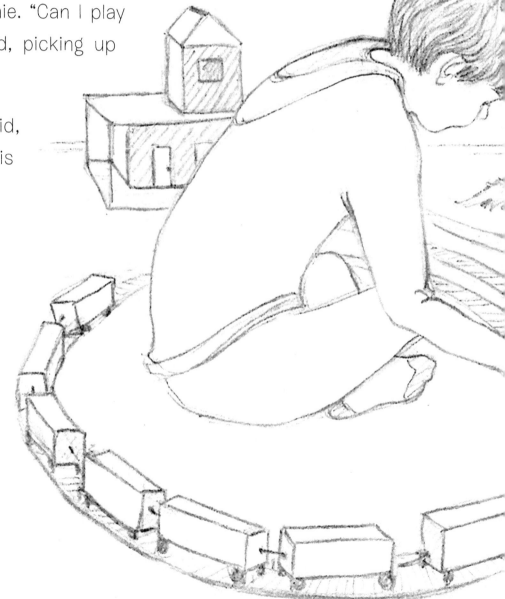

Connor and Sophie spent the next hour playing happily together before he went back to the computer to catch up on the rest of his homework. They even figured out a way to repair the torn wolf.

Which wolf are you feeding?

CPSIA information can be obtained
at www.ICGtesting.com
Printed in the USA
BVHW060141220421
605394BV00008B/1598